# The HAUNTED LIBRARY

FOR
ANDY
—DHB

\* \* \* \* \* \* \* \* \* \* \* \* \* \* \*

## GROSSET & DUNLAP
**Penguin Young Readers Group**
An Imprint of Penguin Random House LLC

Penguin supports copyright. Copyright fuels creativity, encourages diverse voices, promotes free speech, and creates a vibrant culture. Thank you for buying an authorized edition of this book and for complying with copyright laws by not reproducing, scanning, or distributing any part of it in any form without permission. You are supporting writers and allowing Penguin to continue to publish books for every reader.

Text copyright © 2015 by Dori Hillestad Butler. Illustrations copyright © 2015 by Aurore Damant. All rights reserved. Published by Grosset & Dunlap, an imprint of Penguin Random House LLC, 345 Hudson Street, New York, New York 10014. GROSSET & DUNLAP is a trademark of Penguin Random House LLC. Printed in the USA.

Library of Congress Cataloging-in-Publication Data is available.

ISBN 978-0-448-48332-0 (pbk)         10 9 8 7 6 5 4 3 2 1
ISBN 978-0-448-48333-7 (hc)          10 9 8 7 6 5 4 3 2 1

# The HAUNTED LIBRARY
## THE SECRET ROOM

BY DORI HILLESTAD BUTLER
ILLUSTRATED BY AURORE DAMANT

GROSSET & DUNLAP * AN IMPRINT OF PENGUIN RANDOM HOUSE

# GHOSTLY GLOSSARY

### EXPAND
When ghosts make themselves larger

### GLOW
What ghosts do so humans can see them

### HAUNT
Where ghosts live

### PASS THROUGH
When ghosts travel through walls, doors, and other solid objects

### SHRINK
When ghosts make themselves smaller

### SKIZZY
When ghosts feel sick to their stomachs

### SOLIDS
What ghosts call humans

### SPEW
Ghostly vomit

### SWIM
When ghosts move freely through the air

### TRANSFORMATION
When a ghost takes a solid object and turns it into a ghostly object

### WAIL
What ghosts do so humans can hear them

# CHAPTER 1

# TOP SECRET

K az!" Little John called from behind the wall of books. "Kaz, you've got to see this!"

Kaz and Little John were brothers. Ghost brothers. They used to live in an old schoolhouse with the rest of their family. Now they lived in a library with their ghost dog, Cosmo, another ghost named Beckett, a solid girl named Claire, and Claire's family.

Claire could see the ghosts, but no one

else could. Not unless the ghosts were glowing.

"What's back there?" Kaz called to Little John. He knew there was a secret room behind that wall. Beckett often went back there to get away from the solids. But Kaz had never passed through the wall himself.

"Come and see," Little John called back.

"In a minute," Kaz said.

Little John poked his head through the wall of books. "Why 'in a minute'?" he asked. "Why not now?"

Beckett snorted. "Because, Little John, your *big* brother is still scared to pass through a wall."

"I am not!" Kaz protested. He had passed through walls four times already today. He was getting used to it. Sort of. "I just want to wait for Claire.

Otherwise she won't know where I went."

"I don't think Claire will be looking for you anytime soon," Beckett said.

He was probably right. Claire's parents had been away all week at a conference for private detectives. The family had some catching up to do.

"Fine," Kaz said. "I'll show you I'm not scared!"

"Hooray!" Little John cried. His face disappeared from the wall of books.

Kaz's heart went thumpety-thump. He took a deep breath, closed his eyes, and swam into the bookshelf. As the books, the shelf, and the back wall passed through his body, Kaz started to feel skizzy. He pumped his arms and kicked his legs harder and harder . . . until he finally felt himself floating freely in the air again.

Little John giggled. "Open your eyes, Kaz. You're here!"

"Woof! Woof!" Cosmo barked cheerfully.

Kaz opened one eye, then the other. "I did it!" he said with a short laugh. "I passed all the way through to the secret room!"

Beckett drifted through the wall behind Kaz. "I never would've believed it if I hadn't seen it with my own eyes," he said.

Kaz was pretty amazed himself.

"See what I mean about this place?" Little John said as he waved his hand around.

The room was small. And dark. It didn't have any doors or windows. But the most interesting thing about it was that it was full of ghostly objects!

A doll . . . several sets of keys . . .
a catcher's mitt . . . four balls . . . some
socks . . . a strange-looking statue . . .
two teddy bears . . . an old shoe . . .
a yo-yo . . . some books . . . They all
floated there in the air with Kaz, Little
John, Beckett, and Cosmo.

"Where did all this stuff come from?"
Kaz gazed around the room in wonder.

"Different places," Beckett replied.
"A lot of it was here when I moved in.
The rest was left by various ghosts who
have come and gone."

"This looks fun," Little John said as
he picked up a ghostly box. A little crank
stuck through one of the sides.

Little John turned the crank, and
music began to play. All of a sudden,
the top of the box opened and a clown
popped up.

"Ahhh!" Little John and Kaz shrieked.

Beckett laughed. "Are you scaredy-ghosts afraid of a little jack-in-the-box?"

"No!" Little John said, puffing up his chest. "I'm not afraid of anything!"

Cosmo swam over to Kaz and Little John with a ghostly shoe. There was something familiar about that shoe.

"Hey! Is this—" Kaz began.

"It's Finn's shoe!" Little John cried, plucking it from Cosmo's mouth. Finn was Kaz and Little John's big brother. He had accidentally passed through the wall of the old schoolhouse into the Outside about a year ago. Kaz's grandmom and grandpop went after him, but they ended up in the Outside, too.

Then a couple of months ago, some solids came and tore down the old schoolhouse. Kaz, Little John, Mom, Pops,

and Cosmo all ended up in the Outside.
Kaz found Cosmo when he and Claire
were investigating their second case.
Little John had just arrived few days
ago. He traveled inside a library book.
Neither one knew what had happened
to the rest of their family.

"Is this our brother's shoe?" Kaz
asked Beckett. He knew Finn had been
at the library for a while. But that was
long before Kaz got there.

"Could be," Beckett said. "It's hard to
remember where each thing came from."

"I miss Finn," Little John said. "And I
miss Grandmom and Grandpop."

"I miss our whole family," Kaz said.
He wondered if he and Little John would
ever see any of them again. But he didn't
want to think too much about that. It
made him too sad.

"Look at this," Little John said, reaching for a ghostly rag doll.

Kaz could tell by the doll's dress that it was old. It had red yarn for hair, and its eyes, nose, and mouth were sewn on in black thread.

"Remember I told you about that other ghost family I lived with before I came here?" Little John said. "The girl, Kiley, had a doll that blew away. She said it had red hair. And KL could be her initials. Maybe it's hers?"

"I don't know," Beckett said. "That doll has been here a long time."

"Well, she said her doll's been gone for a long time, too," Little John said. He turned to Kaz. "I think I can find their haunt again. Would Claire take us there so we can ask her?"

"Maybe," Kaz said. "But she's busy with her parents right now. Let's look around a little more in here."

Kaz noticed some solid shelves at the back of the room. Each one was crammed full of old wooden crates. They were the only solid things in the whole room. Kaz wafted over to see what was inside the crates.

Not much. Just some old papers and glass bottles. A layer of dirt and spiderwebs covered everything.

As Kaz floated up along the shelving, he noticed an old solid brown envelope lying flat on the top shelf. The words TOP SECRET were scrawled across the front.

"Did you guys see this?" Kaz asked Little John and Beckett as he reached for the envelope. "It says 'Top Secret.'"

"Top Secret?" Little John swam over with the ghost doll.

Holding on to a solid object was still a new skill for Kaz. He couldn't hold the envelope for long. After a few seconds, it slipped through his hands and fell to the floor.

"Do you know what's in there?" Kaz asked Beckett.

"Nope," Beckett said.

"Let's find out!" Little John said as he dived to the floor and grabbed the envelope. He tried to open it, but his hand

passed right through it. He tried again, but this time he dropped it.

Kaz tried, too. He couldn't open it, either.

Even Beckett tried.

None of them could do it. Their hands either passed through the envelope or they dropped it. Every single time.

"Maybe Claire can open it for us," Little John suggested.

"How?" Kaz asked. "It's solid. We can't take solid objects through the wall. And there's no door to this room, so Claire can't come in and open it."

"If you turned it ghostly, you could take it through the wall," Beckett suggested.

Kaz had turned a solid lamp ghostly a few weeks ago, but he had no idea how he'd done it. He'd never been able to turn

another solid object ghostly since. And Beckett didn't know how Kaz had done it, either. He'd never seen a ghost turn an object ghostly before.

"I'll try," Kaz said. He swam down and pressed his hand against the envelope.

Nothing happened.

*Don't think about it. Just do it*, he told himself as he laid his hand on the envelope again.

Still nothing.

Kaz stared at the envelope and concentrated as hard as he could. *Ghostly . . . ghostly . . . ghostly*, he said inside his head. He even tried closing his eyes and whispering, "Ghostly . . . ghostly . . . ghostly . . ."

No matter what Kaz did, the envelope remained solid.

# CHAPTER 2

# A PROBLEM WITH THE GHOST DOLL

**W**as it Kaz's imagination or was someone calling his name? He pressed his ear to the wall that led back to the library craft room and listened.

There it was again. A soft, muffled voice on the other side of the wall. "Kaz? Where are you?"

"Claire?" Kaz called back. "I'm in here."

"You're in the secret room?" Claire's voice was louder now. She'd clearly

moved over to the wall. But her voice still sounded muffled.

Kaz took a deep breath, then swam back through the wall and the bookcase, kicking hard, hard, hard until he was back in the library craft room. Paper cranes dangled from the ceiling above his head.

"Good for you, Kaz!" Claire clapped her hands together. "You passed through the bookshelf! Your ghost skills are getting better every day."

Kaz beamed.

Claire peered at the bookshelf as though she were trying to see through it. "So, what's back there anyway?"

"A whole bunch of ghostly objects," Kaz said as Little John, Cosmo, and Beckett passed through the bookshelf behind him. Little John's arms overflowed with ghostly objects.

"We found our brother Finn's shoe,"
Little John said, holding it up. "And we
found this doll." He held the doll up
next. "I think it belongs to my friend
Kiley. Will you take Kaz and me to her
haunt so we can return it to her?"

"Sure," Claire said as she wandered
the length of the bookshelf.

Little John let go of all the ghostly
objects, except for the doll. "Will
you take us there *now*?" he asked. He

expanded to giant size and placed himself right in front of Claire.

"In a little bit," Claire said, walking around him.

"Why does everyone always say, 'in a little bit'?" Little John moaned.

"Was there any solid stuff back there?" Claire asked Kaz. It was the first time he'd ever heard Claire talk about solid stuff. She normally didn't like that word.

Kaz tried to hide his surprise. "Not much," he said. "Just some old papers and bottles. Oh! And an envelope that says TOP SECRET on it."

"What was in it?" Claire asked.

"We don't know," Kaz said. "We couldn't get it open."

"Kaz tried to turn it ghostly so we could bring it through the wall, but it didn't work," Little John said.

"I wish I could go back there and open it myself," Claire said.

"Can we go find Kiley's haunt now?" Little John asked. "Please? It's not far from here."

"Where is it?" Claire asked.

"You have to walk to the end of the street and through the park. Then turn a corner. It's a big purple house with pink around the windows," Little John said.

"Oh, I know that house," Claire said with a grin. She glanced up at the clock. "It's getting late. My mom might not let me go now. But let's try. Are you guys ready to shrink?" She twisted the top off her water bottle.

"You don't have to take the top off your bottle anymore," Little John said. "Kaz can pass through now."

"Yes, but as long as you've already

taken it off . . . ," Kaz said. He still preferred entering the bottle through an open top rather than passing through the side.

Kaz and Little John shrank down . . . down . . . down . . . but Little John had a problem. He grew smaller, but the doll in his hand did not.

"Hey!" Little John cried as he dangled from the large ghost doll. "Why didn't this doll shrink with me?"

"That's odd," Beckett said, rubbing his chin.

Cosmo sniffed the doll. Then he sniffed the tiny Little John. "Careful, Cosmo," Kaz said, pulling the ghost dog back. "Don't *eat* Little John."

Little John expanded to full size with the doll, then tried shrinking again. The same thing happened. Little John got small. The doll did not.

"Let me try it," Beckett said.

Little John let go of the giant ghost doll and floated over to Kaz. Beckett snatched the doll and shrank down . . . down . . . down . . . until he was the same size as Kaz and Little John.

The doll did not shrink with him.

"Huh. I've never seen that happen before," Beckett said as all three ghosts expanded back to their normal size. Beckett swam around the doll and examined it from all sides.

Little John moaned. "The doll's not going to fit inside your bottle, Claire," he said. "How will we get it back to Kiley?"

Kaz didn't think the doll would fit inside Claire's backpack, either.

Claire bit her lip. Kaz knew that meant she was thinking . . . thinking . . . thinking . . .

All of a sudden, Claire's face lit up. "I have an idea," she said. "I'll be right back."

She ran from the craft room, then returned a few minutes later with a large cardboard box. "We can put the doll in

here," she said as the box dropped to the floor with a plop.

"That'll work," Little John said. "Kaz and I can ride in there, too."

Kaz wasn't sure he wanted to ride inside a cardboard box.

"I'll set the box down right next to the house," Claire said. "Then you guys can pass through the box and into the house like you did when you tried to find the five o'clock ghost."

"What if someone sees you?" Kaz asked Claire. "What if they want to know what's inside the box? Or what if they make you leave, and they want you to take the box with you while we're still inside the house?"

Little John slapped his hand to his head. "Kaz! Do you *always* have to worry about *Every. Little. Thing*?"

"Yes," Kaz said. Because no one else ever worried enough.

Little John shrank down . . . just a bit. Just until he was about the same size as the ghostly rag doll. Then, holding the doll in one arm, he swam inside the box. "Come on, Kaz!" He motioned with his other arm.

Kaz couldn't help but notice that no one had answered his questions. But since no one else was worried, Kaz tried not to worry, either. He shrank down and joined Little John inside the box. Claire closed the flaps over their heads.

Kaz felt the box jolt from side to side as Claire picked it up and started walking across to the library entryway. He heard the door to the Outside open and then Claire yell, "I'm going for a walk!"

"Wait, Claire," her mom called back.

Kaz heard footsteps *click-click-clicking* toward them. "What do you have in that box?" Claire's mom asked.

Kaz couldn't tell whether Claire was still standing inside the library or outside on the front steps.

"Uhhhh . . . ," Claire said.

Kaz and Little John held their breath. If Claire's mom opened the box, she'd see . . . well, nothing. And if they were

outside the library, Kaz, Little John, and the doll would all blow away in the wind!

"It's a science experiment," Claire said finally. Claire's mom liked logic and science. She did NOT like talk about ghosts.

"What kind of science experiment?" Claire's mom asked.

Kaz felt the box shift again in Claire's hands. "Uh . . . I don't want to talk about it until I know whether it works," she said.

"Okay," Claire's mom said. "Be back in an hour. It's almost time for bed."

"I know," Claire promised.

Kaz heard the front door close. He and Little John breathed sighs of relief.

"See, Kaz?" Little John said when they started moving again. "Nothing to worry about."

"For now," Kaz muttered.

# CHAPTER 3
# LITTLE JOHN'S GHOST FRIENDS

**K**az did NOT like traveling inside a cardboard box. He couldn't see anything, so he had no idea where he was.

"Are we almost there?" Kaz called to Claire.

"Almost," she replied. "I see the purple house up ahead."

"I can't wait to see my friends!" Little John said, rubbing his hands together. As he did, his hands started to glow.

Little John made glowing look so easy. It annoyed Kaz that Little John could glow without even thinking about it.

Kaz tried rubbing his own hands together, but nothing happened.

Kaz needed to work on his glowing skills. He knew Claire's grandma could see and hear ghosts when she was Claire's age, but she couldn't see or hear them anymore. Not unless they were glowing or wailing. What if the same thing happened to Claire? If Kaz couldn't glow or wail, and Claire couldn't see or hear him, how could they be friends?

"We're here, you guys," Claire said.

Kaz felt the box hit the ground with a jolt.

"I found a good spot to hide," Claire said. "The box is right up against the house."

"Let's go, Kaz," Little John said as he held tight to the ghost doll and started to pass through the side of the box.

"Wait!" Kaz yanked Little John back by his shirt. "How do you know it's safe to pass through that side? If that's not the side that's up against the house, you'll end up in the Outside!"

"Oh." Little John gulped.

The ghosts felt a *tap! tap! tap!* on one side of the box. It was NOT the same side that Little John had started to pass through. "This is the side you want to go through," Claire said.

*Sometimes it's good to worry,* Kaz thought. *At least a little bit.*

Little John stepped into the side of the box a little more carefully this time. Once Little John was all the way inside the house, Kaz took a deep breath, closed his

eyes, and plunged into the side of the box himself.

Something felt *strange*. The side of the box was all soft and squishy. It felt really different from when he passed through Claire's water bottle. Or the wall of books in the library craft room.

There was also a small gap between the box and the wall of the house. Before Kaz realized what was happening, he felt his head and one arm push through the wall of the house. His middle was in the Outside, between the box and the house. His legs were still inside the box.

And he was *stuck*!

Kaz tried kicking harder, but nothing happened. He tried swimming backward. Still nothing. He opened his eyes and saw his little brother wafting around a fancy living room with the ghost doll. Little John had already expanded to full size.

"Little John!" Kaz called. "Help!"

Little John turned. "Kick harder," he said.

"I am kicking harder!" Kaz cried. "It's not working."

"Try expanding!" Little John said.

Kaz expanded, but that just made his

legs too big for the box. It didn't help him pass the rest of the way through.

Little John let go of the ghost doll and swam toward Kaz. He grabbed on to Kaz's arm with both of his hands and *pullllled*. Kaz kicked harder and Little John *pullllled* harder. Finally, Kaz popped all the way through the box and the wall and landed in the house with Little John.

"Ugh," Kaz said, holding his stomach. "I feel skizzy."

"Well, don't spew," Little John said as he reached for the doll.

"I'll try not to," Kaz said.

Little John swam toward the ceiling. "Come on," he said. "Everyone usually hangs around upstairs in this haunt."

Kaz had never passed through a ceiling before. He looked around and saw a staircase across the room. "I think I'll take the stairs," he said. He didn't feel like passing through any other new objects for a while.

"Okay. I'll see you up there." Little John shot through the ceiling headfirst.

Kaz drifted slowly above the stairs. He wondered if any solids lived in this haunt. He hadn't seen or heard any.

As he floated up and over the top of the banister, he saw and heard other *ghosts.* "Little John! Little John! It's so good to see you again," they all exclaimed as they crowded around Little John. Kaz couldn't tell how many of them there were. They all hugged and kissed Little John like he was *their* long-lost relative.

Kaz felt shy. He hung back by the stairs until Little John called him over. "Kaz, come meet everyone. This is Art, Stretch, and Kiley, and their parents,

Chester and Peg. Everyone, this is my
brother Kaz!"

"Kaz!" Little John's ghost friends swam
over and pumped Kaz's arms. "We're so
happy to meet you! Any brother of Little
John's is a brother of ours!"

"Thanks," Kaz said, backing away just a
bit. Little John's friends sure were friendly.

"Have you reunited with anyone else

in your family, dear?" Peg asked Little John once all the hugging and kissing was over. "Maybe your mother?"

"No." Little John shook his head.

Little John had told Kaz that their mom must have visited this haunt before Little John had arrived. She even left behind a bead from her necklace, so anyone from their family would know she'd been here. Kaz had also found one of her beads in Claire's school, back when he and Claire had solved the case of the ghost backstage. But neither ghost had any idea where their mom was now.

"What's that under your arm, Little John?" Kiley asked.

"Oh!" Little John showed Kiley the ghost doll. "I found it at the library where Kaz and I live now. Is this your missing doll?"

Kiley shook her head. "No."

"Are you sure?" Little John said. "It's got red hair." He ran his fingers through the yarn hair.

"Yes, but Red's hair isn't red like *that*," Kiley said. "And Red isn't a floppy doll."

"Oh." Little John looked disappointed. "Well, do you want it anyway? It's kind of a weird doll. Watch! It doesn't shrink." Little John shrank down . . . down . . . down . . . The ghost doll remained full-size.

"Hmm," Chester said. "You know what that means, don't you?"

"No. What?" Little John asked.

"That doll used to be *solid*," Chester said.

# CHAPTER 4

# SOLID OR GHOSTLY?

Y ou still have the doll," Claire said when she opened the box, and Kaz, Little John, and the doll floated out into the library. "Didn't your friend want it back?"

"It wasn't hers," Little John said.

"But guess what?" Kaz floated beside Claire. "Little John's ghost friends know about transformation!"

Beckett looked up from the book he was reading. "Transformation?"

"That's what it's called when a ghost takes a solid object and turns it into a ghostly object," Kaz said.

"It isn't something any ghost can do," Little John explained. "Chester said, 'A ghost is either born with the ability to transform an object or he's not.'"

"Who's Chester?" Beckett asked with a scowl.

"He's Kiley's dad," Little John said.

"Chester also said that you can tell if a ghostly object was ever solid because it won't shrink," Kaz said. "Let's see if it's true." He wafted over to the ghostly lamp that floated above the table, grabbed hold of it, then shrank down . . . down . . . down . . .

The lamp did not shrink with him.

"Wow!" Claire said. She took her detective's book out of her bag and

opened it to Kaz's page. Then she wrote:
*He can transform objects.*

"I'm not sure it counts if he can't do it on purpose," Beckett grumbled as he read over her shoulder.

Claire wrinkled her nose at him. "You're just jealous that Kaz can do something you can't."

"Hmph," Beckett grunted.

"Chester says it's a very rare skill," Kaz told Beckett. "Very few ghosts have it. Chester only knew about it because his sister Molly had it."

Kaz could hardly believe *he* had it. He just had to figure out how it worked.

Other ghosts, *most* ghosts, simply didn't have the skill to begin with.

"So, once a solid object is transformed into a ghostly object, can it be transformed back to solid form?" Claire asked as she turned a page in her notebook.

Kaz and Little John looked at each other.

"I don't know," Kaz replied. It wasn't a question either of them had thought to ask the other ghost family.

"Chester might not know, either," Little John said. "His sister, Molly, blew away a long time ago. When they were kids. I don't think he knows a lot about transformation."

"I wonder if I'll ever meet a ghost who can teach me about it," Kaz moaned.

"I think you will," Little John said. "We know there's another ghost around who has that skill, too. Unless this doll just floated in by itself one day." He raised the ghostly doll above his head.

"I don't think that doll floated in by itself," Claire said. "Otherwise, how did it end up in the secret room? The ghost who transformed it must have put it there. But who transformed it?"

"And *why* did they transform it?" Kaz asked. "Did they do it on purpose or was it an accident? Like when I transformed the lamp?"

"Maybe it's not such a rare skill after all," Little John said.

"Are you sure you've never met another ghost who could transform

solid objects?" Claire asked Beckett.

"If I did, they didn't tell me about it," Beckett said.

"And you don't remember when that doll got here?" Kaz asked. "Was it here when you moved in?"

"I've been here for twenty years, Kaz," Beckett said. "Do you really expect me to remember what was here then and what wasn't?"

"*I* would remember," Claire said. "Because *I* would write it down." She raised her notebook.

"Hmph," Beckett replied.

"Maybe we should take a closer look at some of the other objects in the secret room," Kaz suggested. "We could try shrinking them and see if any more of them were ever solid."

Claire nodded. "That's a good idea,

Kaz. In fact, you could start with that jack-in-the-box over there." She pointed at the ghostly box that floated in the corner of the room, right where Little John had left it.

"Let me try! Let me try!" Little John swam over, picked up the jack-in-the-box, and shrank down . . . down . . . down . . .

The box did not shrink with him.

Little John expanded back to his usual size. "This was solid, too!" he cried, glowing with excitement. The glow in his body spread through the jack-in-the-box.

"Careful, Little John," Kaz hissed. "You can't just glow in the middle of the room like that. Someone might see you." Someone *solid*, Kaz meant.

"Sorry," Little John said as his glow went out.

"Why don't you guys go back to the secret room and see what else used to be solid?" Claire said.

"Okay!" Little John said. He and Beckett swam toward the back wall.

Kaz hung back. "I wish you could come with us," he said to Claire.

"Me too," she said, forcing a smile. "But I can't. I'm counting on you to tell me everything that happens back there!"

"I will," Kaz promised. Then he passed through the wall.

\* \* \* \* \* \* \* \* \* \* \* \* \* \* \*

Kaz and Little John tried shrinking every single object in the secret room. They sorted the objects into things that shrank and things that didn't. Or things that used to be solid and things that had always been ghostly.

"These keys were solid," Kaz said as he shrank down . . . down . . . down . . . until he was even smaller than the set of keys.

"So were *these* keys," Little John said. He turned a somersault through the ring that held all the keys together.

Even Beckett helped. "These socks were all solid," he said, tossing a handful of socks into a pile with the keys. "But these were not." He tossed another handful of socks onto the other pile.

"Thanks for helping us, Beckett," Kaz said.

"Hmph," Beckett grunted. "It'll take you two all night to do this if I don't help."

He was probably right. There were *a lot* of ghostly objects in the secret room. And it took a lot of ghostly energy to shrink and expand so many times.

A couple of hours later, the ghosts had sorted all the objects. The pile of "used-to-be-solid" objects was way bigger than the pile of "always ghostly" objects.

"Why would a ghost transform all these objects and bring them back here?"

Kaz wondered aloud as he hovered above the "used-to-be-solid" objects. "What was that ghost doing with all this stuff?"

"Who knows?" Little John said as he grabbed the redheaded ghost doll.

And what about the things in the room that were still solid? Kaz wondered. The shelf . . . the crates . . . the papers and glass bottles . . . *the TOP SECRET envelope.* Had those things always been solid? If so, how did they get in there?

Kaz wafted over to the envelope and tried again to turn it ghostly. Just to see if it worked this time.

It didn't.

Kaz sighed. There was still so much to learn about the secret room.

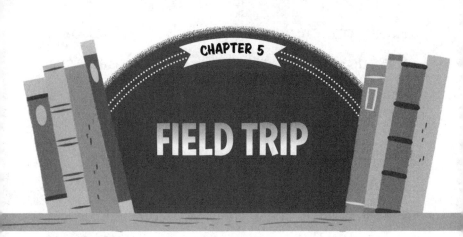

# CHAPTER 5

# FIELD TRIP

A few days later, Claire came home from school and announced, "My class is going on a field trip to the historical society tomorrow. Who wants to come?"

"What's a historical society?" Kaz asked.

"It's a museum," Claire said. "We're going there to learn about the history of our town. Grandma says they'll probably talk about the library because

it's one of the oldest buildings in town."

"Sure, I'll come," Kaz said. If they talked about the library, maybe they'd talk about the secret room.

"I think I'll stay and keep your dog company," Beckett said, giving Cosmo's ears a scratch. "I don't care to venture too far from home."

"And Windy and I will keep *Beckett* company," Little John said as he hugged the redheaded ghost doll.

"Who's Windy?" Claire asked.

"My doll," Little John said. "I named her Windy."

"That's not really *your* doll, Little John," Kaz said.

"Is too! Finders keepers," Little John said, hugging the doll even tighter.

\* \* \* \* \* \* \* \* \* \* \* \* \* \* \*

A lady named Mrs. Roman showed Claire and her classmates around the museum. Kaz hovered above.

"This is what downtown Kirksville, Iowa, looked like in 1910," Mrs. Roman said as she pointed at an old black-and-white photograph.

Kaz had been downtown with Claire many times. It looked different in this photograph. There were no cars on the street, just two horses pulling a wagon.

Mrs. Roman moved down the wall and pointed out some more photographs.

"Here's the old courthouse. And here's an early picture of a house most of you should recognize."

"That's the library!" one of the solid boys shouted out.

Claire stepped forward to get a closer look. Kaz looked over her shoulder.

A sign below the picture said "Walters Mansion. Built 1918."

"She lives there." A solid girl pointed at Claire.

Mrs. Roman smiled. "You must be Karen Lindstrom's granddaughter."

Claire nodded.

"Well, you're a very lucky girl," Mrs. Roman said. "You live in one of the most famous houses in Kirksville! People used to come from all over to see it."

"Why is it so famous?" the boy next to Claire asked.

"Because it's big," said a girl in the back.

"And old," said another girl.

"When it was first built, no one around here had ever seen such a mansion before," Mrs. Roman explained. "It still looks pretty impressive today, wouldn't you agree?"

The kids all nodded.

"A man named Martin Walters built it as a gift to his wife," Mrs. Roman said.

"That's some gift," the boy next to Claire said. "Here, have a house!"

Several kids snickered.

"It was indeed 'some gift,'" Mrs. Roman

said. "Especially when you consider the Walters didn't have children to fill all those rooms. But one thing Martin Walters did have was money."

"Where'd he get so much money?" asked the girl in the back.

"I'll show you," Mrs. Roman said. She led the students to another display inside the museum. The sign on the wall read "Walters Bottling Company."

There were even more black-and-white photographs on this wall. And lots of old bottles stacked in crates on the floor.

"Hey, there were bottles like that in the secret room," Kaz told Claire.

"Martin Walters established Walters Bottling Company back in 1900," Mrs. Roman explained. "And he created a whole new kind of soda pop he called Walters Brew. That's how he made his fortune."

"What did it taste like?" asked a boy in a blue jacket.

"We think it may have been similar to root beer," Mrs. Roman said. "But no one today really knows for sure."

"Why not?" asked a girl in the back.

"Well, Mr. Walters refused to tell anyone what was in it," Mrs. Roman said. "He promised one day his secret recipe would be revealed. To the right person

58

under the right circumstances. But that day never came."

"So where is the recipe?" asked the boy in the blue jacket. "Is it in the library somewhere?"

"Oh, I don't think so," Mrs. Roman said. "Everyone in town knows how important a discovery like that would be to the historical society. I would hope that if someone ever found the recipe, they'd bring it to us. But I don't think that will ever happen. I suspect the recipe was never written down. We'll probably never know what was in it."

Kaz and Claire exchanged a look. Was *that* what was inside the envelope in the secret room? The recipe for Walters Brew?

If only Kaz could open the envelope or transform it and bring it through the wall. Then they could find out.

* * * * * * * * * * * * * * * * *

Claire walked slowly along the bookshelf at the back of the library craft room. "There's got to be a way into that secret room," she said.

"There is," Beckett said. "Through the wall!"

"I mean, there's got to be a way people who aren't *ghosts* can get in," Claire said. "A secret passageway or something. Otherwise, how did Martin Walters get back there? How did he hide his secret soda-pop recipe in there?" She pushed against the bookshelf and felt around all the books.

"What makes you so sure he did?" Beckett asked.

Kaz and Claire had told Beckett and Little John about their trip to the historical society. But Beckett wasn't as convinced

as they were that the long-lost soda-pop recipe was inside that envelope.

"What else could be in there?" Kaz asked.

Beckett shrugged. "Could be anything. It could be the recipe. It could be something else. I thought you two were detectives. Detectives don't jump to conclusions before getting the facts."

"We're not!" Claire said. "I *think* the recipe is inside that envelope, but we won't know for sure until we can open it. That's why I need to get into the secret room!" She started removing books from the shelves and piling them on the table in the middle of the room.

"Claire!" A voice startled everyone. It was Claire's mom. She stood in the doorway with her hands on her hips. "What are you doing?"

# CHAPTER 6

# WHO ELSE LIVED AT THE LIBRARY?

Grandma Karen came up behind Claire's mom. "What's going on?" She glanced curiously at Claire's mom and then toward the stack of books on the table.

"I'm looking for a passageway to a secret room," Claire said. "We learned about Martin Walters at the historical society today. He's the one who built this house. He got the money to build it by inventing a new kind of soda pop. But no one knows where the recipe for the soda pop is. *I* think it's back there." She banged the wall with her fist.

Claire's mom marched over to the table, grabbed an armload of books, and put them back on the shelf. "Trust me, Claire. It's *not* back there," she said firmly. "There's no secret room in this house."

Grandma Karen looked surprised by Claire's mom's strong reaction. "I don't know, Katherine," she said. "I think there *could* be a small room back there. I thought so back when we used to live here. If you walk around outside and look at where the window is and where the corner of the house is—"

"Wait," Claire interrupted. "What do you mean '*when we used to live here*'?"

Neither Claire's mom nor Grandma Karen answered Claire at first.

"I knew you guys lived in this town when Mom was a little girl," Claire pressed. "But did you actually live *here*?"

"Yes, we did," Grandma Karen said. "This was an apartment house for many, many years. And our apartment was right here. This craft room was our living room, bedroom, and kitchen. The bathroom was down the hall. Right where it still is. We shared it with another apartment."

"This little room was your whole apartment?" Claire cried.

"That's right," Grandma Karen said.

"Why didn't you ever tell me?" Claire asked, her eyes flicking back and forth between her mom and her grandma.

"It wasn't a secret," her mother said as she grabbed another armload of books from the table. "I just don't like to talk about those days. It wasn't a happy time."

Grandma Karen pulled out a chair and sat down. She motioned for Claire to do the same. "I was a single mom," Grandma Karen began. "We struggled to make ends meet. But even though times were tough, I always *loved* this house. Isn't it the most beautiful house you've ever seen?"

"It is nice," Claire agreed.

Claire's mom banged more books against the shelf.

"Sylvia always took such good care of it," Grandma Karen said. "Sylvia was the previous owner. When she put the house on the market, I couldn't resist buying it. Even though I knew I didn't want to

manage an apartment house. But by then all the renters had moved out. And the library needed more space, so I decided to lease the downstairs to the city for a library. There was still too much space upstairs for me alone. But then you and your parents moved in, and, well, things have a way of working out, don't they?" Grandma Karen patted Claire's arm.

"I guess," Claire said.

"You know," Grandma Karen said, looking thoughtful. "If you want to hear more about this house, Sylvia lived here for more than forty years. You've probably seen her in the library. She's an

older lady. She often wears fancy jewelry."

"Yeah, I think I've seen her," Claire said.

"I think we found her lost earring once," Kaz told Claire.

"Nobody knows more about the history of this house than Sylvia Lock," Grandma Karen said. "Tomorrow's Saturday. Why don't I write down her address for you, and you can pay her a visit? Ask her if she knows anything about a secret room."

"Mother!" Claire's mom said sharply.

"What, Katherine?" Grandma Karen asked.

Claire's mom's jaw tightened. "I don't think that's a good idea," she said.

"You don't think it's a good idea for Claire to visit a lonely woman?" Grandma Karen asked. "Why in the world not?"

But Claire's mom couldn't come up with a reason.

\* \* \* \* \* \* \* \* \* \* \* \* \* \* \*

"Can Windy and I come with you this time?" Little John asked when Kaz and Claire got ready to go visit Mrs. Lock the next day.

"You can come," Kaz replied. "But there isn't room for Windy in Claire's bottle."

"Can't we take the box?" Little John asked.

"No!" Kaz said. "I'm not traveling inside a box just so you can bring a doll."

Little John sighed. "Will you take care of Windy while I'm gone?" he asked Beckett.

"Hmph," Beckett said as he took the doll from Little John.

Kaz and Little John shrank down . . . down . . . down . . . and passed through Claire's water bottle. Then they set off for Mrs. Lock's house.

"My mom was acting weird yesterday," Claire said along the way.

"She sure was," Kaz said from inside the water bottle.

"Why would she think visiting Mrs. Lock wasn't a good idea?" Claire asked.

"I don't know your mom very well," Little John said. "But even I thought that was weird."

When they got to Mrs. Lock's house, Claire went up the steps and rang the bell.

Mrs. Lock opened her door a crack. "Yes?" she said.

"Hi. I'm Claire Kendall," Claire said cheerfully. "I live at the library."

"Yes," Mrs. Lock said again. She didn't open her door any wider.

"I have some questions about the library. About the building, I mean. My grandma said you probably know more about it than anyone."

Mrs. Lock blushed. "I suppose I do,"

she said. "Come in." She opened her door all the way, then quickly closed it again behind Claire. "Please take off your shoes."

"Why do we have to take off our shoes?" Little John asked.

"*We* don't," Kaz said. "She's not talking to us, because she can't see us. And we don't walk on the floor, anyway. She wants Claire to take off her shoes because she doesn't want Claire to bring dirt in."

"Ohhhh," said Little John.

While Claire bent over to untie her shoes, Kaz and Little John passed through the water bottle and expanded to full size. It was getting easier to pass through a solid object every time Kaz did it. He hardly even felt skizzy anymore. And he had to admit, it was nice to pass through the bottle without having to wait for Claire to open the top.

Mrs. Lock pointed at a tall brown chair near the fireplace. "Sit down. Would you like some tea?"

"No, thank you," Claire said as she sat down and pulled out her notebook. "Do you know anything about a secret room or any secret passageways in the library?"

"Secret rooms and secret passageways. Oh, wouldn't that be fun!" Mrs. Lock chuckled. "No, I'm afraid I don't."

"Are you sure?" Claire asked. "What about behind that bookshelf in the craft room? My grandma says there's extra space between that wall and the outside wall. Couldn't there be a secret room in that space?"

Mrs. Lock thought for a minute. "I know the area you're talking about," she said. "I wanted to take that back wall out so the apartment would be larger. But the

fellow who did the work for me advised against it."

"Why?" Claire asked.

"You know, I don't quite remember." Mrs. Lock scratched her head. "But if you really want to know, you could probably ask him. His name is Victor Helsing, and he lives in that nursing home over on Valley Street. He did all of the remodeling. If there was ever a secret room or a secret passageway in that house, he's the one who would know about it."

# CHAPTER 7

# MORE GHOSTS!

Kaz and Little John had never been inside a nursing home before. A large yellow, green, and blue bird greeted them from its cage beside the door when Claire walked in. "Hello! Hello!" the bird squawked.

"Hello," Claire said to the bird. "What's your name?"

"Hello! Hello!" the bird squawked again.

As soon as the front door closed, Kaz

and Little John passed through the side of Claire's water bottle and expanded to normal size.

"I never knew birds could talk," Kaz said as he drifted close, but not *too* close, to the cage.

"His name is Petey," a lady behind a counter said to Claire. "Ask him who's a pretty bird."

"Who's a pretty bird?" Claire asked Petey.

The bird shifted on his perch. He didn't say anything.

"Who's a pretty bird, Petey?" the lady at the desk said.

"Shut up!" the bird squawked.

"Petey!" the lady exclaimed as Claire, Kaz, and Little John giggled.

"Petey!" the bird repeated.

The lady at the desk shook her head

in dismay. "Can I help you?" she asked Claire.

"I'd like to see Victor Helsing," Claire said, leaning on the counter.

"Sure," said the lady. "He's in room 105. Go down that hallway and walk through the activity room. It'll be the first room on the right."

"Thanks," Claire said as she, Kaz, and Little John started down the hall.

"Hey, there's a ghost!" Little John pointed up ahead.

"Two of them," Kaz said, as first one, then two ghosts darted across the hall from one room into another. Neither of the ghosts was glowing. And neither of them noticed Kaz or Little John.

Claire, Kaz, and Little John continued down the hall and into the activity room. They were surprised to find four *more* ghosts hovering above a table where four solids were playing cards.

"Hey! Who are you guys?" Little John asked as he and Kaz swam over to the

ghosts. They were all lady ghosts. *Old* lady ghosts. The ladies turned to Little John and Kaz.

The solids turned, too.

"Who are *you* guys?" a solid lady with bluish hair asked.

Kaz stared. Was that solid lady talking to him and Little John? She had to be. She said *you guys* and she was looking right at them. Claire was still halfway across the room. She had stopped to pull out her notebook.

"We don't usually see such young ghosts in here," said the solid lady who sat across from the blue-haired lady.

"Can you see us?" Kaz asked the solid ladies. Neither he nor Little John was glowing.

"Of course we can see you," said a solid man who sat between the two ladies.

"We may be old, but we're not blind," said the other solid man.

"You mean *all* of you can see us?" Little John cried, wide-eyed.

"Almost everyone in this nursing home can see us," said one of the ghost ladies. "Everyone of a certain age, I mean."

"Little John? Kaz? Is that you?" said a voice behind them.

Kaz and Little John turned. "GRANDMOM?!?!" they cried out. Grandpop was there, too.

The four ghosts swam to each other. First Kaz and Grandmom hugged while Little John and Grandpop hugged. Then Kaz and Grandpop hugged while Little John and Grandmom hugged.

"How marvelous! It's a family reunion," said one of the ghost ladies.

"Is Finn here, too?" Little John asked.

"No," Grandmom replied. "I'm afraid we never found him. What are you two doing here?"

But before Kaz or Little John could explain, Grandmom grabbed them both and hugged them again. "I didn't think we'd ever see you again!"

"I . . . didn't think . . . we'd ever . . . see . . . *you* . . . again, either!" Kaz said, gasping for air.

Grandpop tugged on Grandmom's arm. "Let the poor child catch his breath," he said.

"Sorry, sorry," Grandmom said as she finally let Kaz and Little John go.

Claire cleared her throat. "Kaz? Are you going to introduce us?" she asked.

Grandpop peered down at Claire. "Who is this solid child?" he asked. "How does she know your name?"

"Can she see us when we're not glowing?" Grandmom asked.

"Yes," Kaz replied. "Grandmom, Grandpop, this is Claire. She's my friend."

"Pleased to meet you," Claire said as she offered a hand.

Grandmom and Grandpop each touched their ghost hands to Claire's solid hand. It was the closest they could come to shaking hands.

"Are you having trouble finding Mr. Helsing's room?" the solid lady from the front desk asked Claire as she wheeled a cart into the activity room. She wheeled it right through Grandmom. "Room 105 is over here. Come with me. I'll introduce you."

Claire looked torn. She clearly wanted to go talk to Mr. Helsing. But she also wanted to stay with Kaz and

Little John and their grandparents.

"Go ahead," Kaz told her. "We'll be here when you're done talking to Mr. Helsing."

Claire nodded and hurried away with the lady from the desk.

Kaz couldn't tell whether his grandparents approved of Claire or not. Kaz's family had always warned him to stay away from solids.

"Claire's really nice," Kaz told his grandparents.

"She is." Little John backed him up.

"She would never hurt a ghost," Kaz went on. "She helps ghosts. She's been trying to help me find our family."

"It's okay, Kaz," Grandpop said. "We're glad you met a nice solid girl. We've met some nice solids here in the nursing home, too."

"Yes, we may have been wrong about the solids," Grandmom said. "The ones we've met have all been very lovely. But we want to hear about you two. What are you doing here? Why aren't you at our haunt?"

Kaz and Little John exchanged a look. Grandmom and Grandpop blew into the Outside before their haunt was torn down. They didn't know their haunt was *gone*.

So Kaz and Little John told their grandparents about the big trucks that came with a wrecking ball and destroyed the old schoolhouse.

Grandmom put her hand to her chest as she listened. "Where is everyone?" she asked. "Where are your mom and dad?"

"We don't know," Kaz said. "We all got separated."

Kaz told them how the wind had blown him into the library. Little John told them how the wind had blown him into a barn, then into another haunt where he met Kiley and her family.

"We haven't seen Mom or Dad since our haunt was torn down," Little John said.

"But we found beads from Mom's necklace," Kaz said. He reached into his pocket and pulled out a tiny ghost bead. "Little John has one, too!"

Little John showed Grandmom and Grandpop his ghost bead.

"Kiley's mom and dad told me they'd heard there were ghosts in the library, so I tried and tried to swim in there, but the wind kept blowing me down the street," Little John said. "Then I got the idea to hide inside a library book. That's how I finally got into the library!"

"That was very clever of you," Grandmom said.

"I know!" Little John replied. "And brave, too!"

"Oh, brother," Kaz said, rolling his eyes.

"We've had quite a time these past few months, too," Grandpop said. "We tried to find Finn, but the wind kept blowing us off course. One day it blew us in here. And, well . . . we like it here, so we've decided to stay."

"These solids have some wonderful stories," Grandmom said. "And we love all the activities. There's movie night. Music. Card games. We've never had so much fun!"

Kaz was glad his grandparents had found such a nice new haunt.

A little while later, Claire came back.

"Mr. Helsing fell asleep on me," she told the ghosts. "But that's okay. We should head back to the library, anyway. Are you ready?"

"I need to ask these ghosts one more question first," Kaz said. "Do any of you know about transformation?"

"Transformation?" The four ghost ladies all looked confused.

"You know. Turning solid objects into ghostly objects," Little John said, swimming forward. "Kaz can do it!"

"Well," Kaz spoke up. "I did it once. But I don't know how I did it."

A strange look passed between Grandmom and Grandpop.

"So, it's true," Grandmom said.

"What's true?" Little John asked.

"You boys have to understand," Grandpop said. "That's such a rare skill that most ghosts aren't even sure it's real. My uncle Benjamin claimed he had the skill, but no one ever saw him transform anything. We thought it was all talk. But if you have the skill, too, Kaz . . ."

"I may have the skill, but I don't know how it works," Kaz said. "Do you guys?"

Kaz's grandparents shook their heads sadly.

"I was hoping you could tell us how it works," Grandpop said.

Kaz sighed.

Claire checked the time on her phone. "You'll figure it out, Kaz. I know you will. But if I'm not back at the library soon, I'm going to get in trouble." She held out her water bottle.

Kaz and Little John started to shrink down . . . down . . . but Grandmom interrupted them mid-shrink. "Wait! You boys aren't going with her, are you?"

"Of course not," Grandpop said, grabbing each boy by the arm. "Now that we're all together again, they're staying right here with us."

## CHAPTER 8

# FAMILY TROUBLES

N o!" Little John cried. "I don't want to stay here. I want to go back to the library. Windy and Cosmo are there. We can't leave Cosmo. We can't leave Beckett, either. He'll be lonely without us."

"Who's Beckett?" Grandpop asked.

"He's the other ghost who lives at the library," Kaz said.

"He's old. Like you," Little John added.

"Little John!" Kaz nudged his brother. "That's not polite."

"Oh, that's okay, Kaz," Grandmom said with a smile. "We know we're old."

"Why don't you and Grandpop come to the library with us?" Kaz said. "We'll have to shrink really small to fit inside Claire's bottle. But there's plenty of room for all of us at the library."

Grandmom turned to Grandpop. "I like it here," she said. "I don't want to go someplace else."

"Well, we like it at the library," Little John said.

"I don't mean to eavesdrop," said the blue-haired solid lady. "But I think you should let those ghost children go back to the library with their friend. They want to be with people their own age."

"And you two should stay here with us," said one of the ghost ladies.

"I promise I'll take good care of Kaz and Little John," Claire told Grandmom and Grandpop. "And so will Beckett. I'll bring them back here to visit you. Every day, if you want! Please?"

"Pleeeease?" begged Kaz and Little John.

"Well," Grandmom said. "I suppose they've gotten along on their own this long."

"And it sounds like they have a responsible ghost adult looking out for them," Grandpop added.

"If you promise to come back and visit

often, you can go with your friend,"
Grandmom said.

"Hooray!" Kaz, Little John, and Claire
cheered.

"Don't ever tell your parents we
allowed this," Grandmom said.

"Deal," Kaz said.

On the way home, Kaz asked Claire,
"Did Mr. Helsing tell you why he didn't
want Mrs. Lock to knock down that wall
in the library? Does he know about the
secret room?"

"He said that wall was a main support for the rest of the house," Claire said. "That's why it couldn't be removed. He didn't know anything about any secret rooms or secret passageways in the house."

Kaz groaned. He, Claire, and Little John were no closer to getting the Top Secret envelope out of the secret room. They were no closer to getting Claire *into* the secret room, either.

But they had found their grandparents! That was something.

\* \* \* \* \* \* \* \* \* \* \* \* \* \* \* \*

Claire's mom was waiting in the entryway when Claire returned to the library. She leaped to her feet as soon as Claire opened the door. "Have you been visiting with Mrs. Lock all this time?" she asked.

"Not the whole time," Claire said

as she closed the door behind her.

Kaz and Little John passed through Claire's water bottle and expanded to full size. Little John swam over to get his doll back from Beckett.

Claire's mom followed Claire across the entryway. "So, what did you and Mrs. Lock talk about?" she asked. She seemed more interested in Mrs. Lock than she was in where else Claire might have gone.

"Did she say anything about a secret passageway or a secret room?" Claire's mom asked. "Does she think that old soda-pop recipe is somewhere in this house?"

"I didn't ask her about the recipe," Claire said. "I only asked about the secret room."

"What did she say?" Claire's mother stood so close to her and stared so

hard at her that Claire was obviously uncomfortable.

"She doesn't think there is one," Claire said, hanging up her coat.

Claire's mom's shoulders relaxed.

"Are you okay, Mom?" Claire peered at her mother. "You're acting so weird."

Claire's mom ran her hand through her hair. "I don't know what you mean," she said.

"Well, you didn't really want me to go visit Mrs. Lock. And now you're asking lots of questions."

"I'm your mother," she said with a nervous laugh. "I get to ask questions."

"Yeah, but you're asking more questions than you usually do."

Claire's mom turned away. "Do you have homework?" she asked.

Claire clucked her tongue. "And now you're changing the subject!"

"I'm changing the subject because the subject is finished," her mom said. "Can you say the same for your homework?"

"No," Claire admitted. "Fine, I'll go do it." She shouldered her backpack and headed toward the craft room.

But her mom stopped her in her tracks. "I really wish you wouldn't always do your homework in the craft room. Can't you do it upstairs?"

Claire turned. "What's wrong with doing it in the craft room?"

"Must you argue?" Claire's mom asked in a tired voice. "Can't you just do as I ask?"

"Fine," Claire said with a huff. "I'll do it upstairs."

"What's the matter with your mom?" Kaz asked as he drifted beside Claire. Little

John followed close behind with Windy.

"I have no idea," Claire replied under her breath.

"I'm going to find out," Little John said. He turned a somersault and swam after Claire's mom. He got right in front of her so she could see him. Then, slowly, he started to glow. The glow spread through his body and into the doll.

"Little John! No!" Kaz cried, swimming over.

Claire ran after the ghosts.

"Why . . . are . . . you . . . acting . . . so . . . weird . . .?" Little John wailed at Claire's mom.

There was no doubt Claire's mom could see and hear Little John. "Wh-wh-who are you?" she stammered. "What are you doing here? And *what* are you doing with that doll?"

Claire sighed. "I hate to break it to you, Mom. But there are ghosts in this library. This one's name is Little John. Little John, meet my mom."

"Hello . . . ," Little John wailed.

"What are you doing with that doll?" Claire's mom said again. She pointed at the doll that glowed in Little John's arms.

"Ohhhh!" Kaz gasped. "I don't know why we didn't figure it out before!"

"Figure what out?" Claire asked Kaz right in front of her mom.

"What's your mom's name, Claire?" Kaz asked. "It's Katherine, isn't it? Your grandma called her Katherine. Could KL stand for Katherine Lindstrom?" He pointed at the letters on the doll's dress.

Claire turned to her mom. "This is *your* doll!"

# CHAPTER 9

# CLAIRE'S MOM'S SECRET

Yes. That's my Sophie," Claire's mom said. She couldn't take her eyes off the doll.

"Sophie . . . ?" Little John wailed. "I . . . call . . . her . . . Windy . . ." He hugged the doll tight and turned to Kaz. "Do I have to give her back?"

"Well," Kaz said in a voice that only Claire and the other ghosts could hear. He wasn't sure what to say. As soon as Little John let the doll go, it would stop glowing.

Claire's mom wouldn't be able to see it. But it was still hers, not Little John's.

"How did you get my doll?" Claire's mom demanded.

"I . . . found . . . her . . . in . . . the . . . secret . . . room . . ." It took a lot of energy for a ghost to both glow and wail at the same time. Especially when that glow also filled another object. Little John couldn't help it. Eventually his glow went out.

Claire's mom blinked. "Where'd he go?" she asked, looking all around.

"He's still here," Claire said. "He's just not glowing anymore. There are two other ghosts here, too. My friend Kaz, who can't glow." Kaz waved even though he knew Claire's mom couldn't see him. "And Beckett. I don't know if Beckett can glow. Can you, Beckett?"

"I choose not to," Beckett said.

"Glowing is what ghosts do when they want us to see them," Claire told her mom.

"I know what glowing is," Claire's mom said dismissively. "What I *want* to know is where is that ghost and what did he do with my doll?"

Claire tilted her head. "How do you know about glowing?"

Just then, Grandma Karen came into the library entryway. Cosmo swam behind her. "What's going on out here?" she asked.

"Where are you, you ghost?" Claire's mom asked as she walked around the entryway and peered into all the dark corners. "Come out and glow so I can see you!"

Little John and the doll glowed again, but not as brightly as before. "It's . . . *hard* . . . to . . . keep . . . glowing . . . ," he wailed.

Claire's mom's finger shot out. "There!" she cried, right before Little John and the doll stopped glowing again. "Did you see that, Mother? Did you see what that ghost was holding?"

Grandma Karen took two steps toward Little John, but she couldn't see him or the doll anymore, either. "It looked a lot like the doll my mother made for you," she said with surprise. "The one you lost when you were about nine years old."

Claire's mom shook her head. "I didn't

lose it, Mother," she said. "A ghost took it. And now *another* ghost has it."

Grandma Karen looked even *more* surprised. She scratched her chin. Kaz could almost see her piecing something together. "Katherine?" she said after a little while. "Did you see ghosts when you were a child?"

Claire gasped. "Did you, Mom?"

Her mom hesitated for a couple of seconds, then she nodded.

"YOU SAW GHOSTS, TOO?" Claire

cried at the same time as Grandma Karen said, "Why didn't you ever tell me?"

Claire's mom opened her mouth, but no words came out.

"Let's sit down," Grandma Karen said as she led Claire's mom over to the bench. Claire plopped down between them. Kaz, Little John, Beckett, and Cosmo hovered nearby.

"I saw ghosts when I was a child, too," Grandma Karen said.

"You did?" Claire's mom shifted on the bench. "Why didn't *you* ever tell *me*?"

Grandma Karen smiled. "I don't know. I certainly would have if I'd had any idea you saw them, too."

"I tried to tell you about the ghosts I saw when I first started seeing them in Seattle," Claire said as she hugged her knees to her chest. "I tried to tell you here, too. But you always say, 'no ghost talk.'"

"I know, honey," Claire's mom replied. "And maybe that was a mistake. It's not normal to see ghosts. I didn't want the kids at school to tease you. I also don't want you to spend time with ghosts. Ghosts are dangerous!"

"Dangerous!" Beckett wailed.

"You . . . solids . . . are . . . far . . . more . . . dangerous . . . than . . . we . . . are . . . !"

"Who said that?" Claire's mom whirled around.

"That's Beckett," Claire said. "Beckett, say hello to my mom and grandma."

"Hmph," Beckett said in a voice that Claire's mom and grandma couldn't hear.

Claire's mom leaned back against the wall. "Let me tell you about the ghosts I saw when I was your age, Claire. They all lived here in this apartment house. The first one I met was a girl named Molly."

*Molly?* Kaz and Little John glanced at each other.

"That was Chester's sister's name!" Little John said. "Did Chester's sister end up *here* when she blew away from their haunt?"

Kaz was wondering that, too.

"Molly was my friend," Claire's mom continued. "She had a very unique ability among ghosts. She could make things disappear from the solid world!"

"It has to be the same Molly," Little John said with growing excitement.

Kaz agreed.

"Kaz can transform objects, too," Claire said.

"Can he?" Claire's mom asked.

"Well—" Kaz said, squirming a little.

"It doesn't count if he can't do it on command!" Beckett said.

"So, what happened to Molly?" Little John asked. "She's not here now."

"Let's listen and maybe we'll find out," Kaz said.

"I don't know about Kaz, but Molly liked to transform things like socks and keys. As a joke," Claire's mom said with

a smile. "Sometimes she took toys from kids who lived here. Especially if those kids teased me. But she always returned them to the solid world. Eventually."

*So it is possible to return a ghostly object to the solid world*, Kaz thought.

"I don't understand why you want Claire to stay away from the ghosts, Katherine," Grandma Karen said. "Molly seems like a perfectly nice ghost friend."

"She was. But then another ghost blew in," Claire's mom said. Her smile fell. "Her name was Annie, and she was a nasty, nasty ghost. She wanted Molly to transform *everything* in every apartment in the whole house. Even the furniture. She wanted the people who lived here to get scared and move out so the ghosts could have the whole place to themselves."

"That's not very nice," Claire said.

"When Molly refused, Annie got very angry," Claire's mom said. "She PUSHED Molly through the wall. I ran outside to try to help Molly, but there was nothing I could do. I never saw her again."

"Ohhh," Claire said with sympathy.

"When I came back inside," Claire's mom went on, "Annie had gathered up all the things that Molly had transformed, including *my doll*. She took them back behind that wall, where the secret room is. And she said that if I, or anyone else, ever

went near that room, she'd do something *really* terrible. That's why I didn't want you to visit Mrs. Lock, Claire. I wasn't sure what she knew about the secret room. And I didn't want her to encourage you to go poking around back there."

"So you do know about the secret room," Claire said.

Her mom nodded. "I don't know what's back there, but you have to stay away from that wall, Claire. We don't want any ghosts to hurt us."

"Oh, honey," Grandma Karen said, taking Claire's mom's hand. "These ghosts aren't going to hurt us."

"That's right," Claire agreed. "And you don't have to worry about Annie. She's not even here anymore. Is she?" she asked her ghost friends.

"No," Kaz and Little John said.

"I've never met a ghost named Annie," Beckett said.

"Beckett says he's never met a ghost named Annie here," Claire told her mother. "And he's been here forever. All the ghosts who live here are nice ghosts. Really!"

"You said your friend Kaz could transform objects, too," Claire's mom said as she tucked a piece of hair behind her ear. "Is he nice enough to transform my doll back?"

"He's definitely nice enough to do it," Claire said. "But he doesn't know how to do it. He's only transformed something once and that was a total accident."

"Oh," Claire's mom said. "Well, maybe I can help with that. I know how Molly's ability worked."

# CHAPTER 10

# TRANSFORMATION

The secret is in the tip of your thumb and your second finger," Claire's mom said to the wall beside Kaz.

Kaz wished he could glow so Claire's mom could see him when she spoke to him.

"You have to touch the very tip of your thumb and your second finger to whatever it is you want to transform, and then quickly pull your hand away." Claire's mom demonstrated with her

own hand. "That's what pulls the solid out of the object. *If* you're a ghost that has the ability to transform an object."

"Try it, Kaz," Claire urged. "See if you can transform that leaf on the floor."

Kaz dived down to a leaf that had fallen from the plant in the corner.

"Remember, just the tip of your thumb and your second finger," Claire's mom said again as all eyes focused on Kaz. And the leaf.

Kaz slowly picked up the leaf. He held it between his thumb and second finger and then let go.

The leaf remained solid as it fluttered back to the floor.

"I think you have to let go faster," Claire suggested.

"And don't squeeze it too tight," Claire's mom said. "You need to hold it kind of loose. Molly used to sort of balance things on the tips of her fingers, then flick her hand away!"

Kaz reached for the leaf again. But this time he had such a light hold that it fell to the floor before he could even try to transform it.

Grandma Karen groaned.

"Keep trying, Kaz," Claire said.

Kaz sighed as he picked up the leaf again and held it gently, gently, gently. So gently that it sort of hovered there in the air between his thumb and his second finger. Then he quickly flicked his hand away as he let the leaf go.

Kaz stared in amazement as the leaf turned ghostly!

"You did it!" Claire clapped her hands

together. Her mom and Grandma Karen smiled.

"Yay! Kaz!" Little John exclaimed.

Even Beckett looked impressed.

"Now tell him to put it back." Claire's mom leaned forward on the bench. "Then ask him to see if he can bring my doll back, too." She was growing more and more excited.

"He can hear you, Mom," Claire said. "He's right here."

"I don't know if I can transform it back," Kaz said as he grabbed the ghostly leaf. "I don't know how that works."

"Did Molly tell you how she made things solid again?" Claire asked her mom.

Kaz turned the leaf all around. He tried squeezing it between his thumb and first finger. *Wait! Second finger, not first,* he said

to himself as he switched his hold. And just like that, the leaf turned solid again!

"Looks like he figured it out," Claire's mom said.

Kaz turned the leaf ghostly again. Then solid. Then ghostly. Then solid. "I think I've got it!" He giggled.

Little John brought the ghost doll over to Kaz. "Go ahead and transform Windy," he said glumly. "She belongs to Claire's mom. Not me."

"Thanks, Little John," Claire said. "I've probably got another doll around somewhere that you can have."

"Okay," Little John said.

Kaz squeezed his two thumbs and two second fingers around the doll's middle.

The doll turned solid, then fell to the floor.

Claire's mom lunged for it. "Oh, thank you," she said, looking somewhere between Kaz and Little John. "Thank you! Thank you!"

While Claire and her mom and grandma exclaimed over the doll, Kaz said, "I know what I should transform now."

Little John perked up. "The envelope in the secret room!"

The ghosts raced to the craft room and sailed through the bookshelf at the back of the room.

Kaz swam over to the envelope and picked it up. He held it with the very tip of his thumb and second finger, then quickly flicked his hand away.

The envelope turned ghostly!

"Aha! Now we can open it and see what's inside," Little John cried as he reached for the envelope.

"No." Kaz snatched it away. "*Now* we can take it through the wall." Holding tight to the envelope, Kaz turned and swam through the wall.

Little John groaned.

"Back already?" Claire said as the three ghosts returned to the craft room.

Her eyes widened at the envelope in Kaz's hand. "Is the recipe inside?"

"I don't know," Kaz said. "I think you should be the one to open it." He squeezed the envelope with the tip of his thumb and second finger, and the envelope turned solid and dropped to the floor.

Claire's mom and Grandma Karen gathered around as Claire picked up the envelope.

"Wow, you even transformed the dust," Claire said, brushing the dust away with her hand. She slipped her finger under the flap, tore the envelope open, and pulled out two very thin, faded papers that crinkled in her hands.

The top paper was a letter. "It's kind of hard to read," Claire said, squinting at it.

Kaz tried to read over her shoulder, but he couldn't make out the words at all. He'd never seen such strange writing before.

Claire managed to muddle through it. Slowly. "'August 14, 1928,'" she read. "'To Whom It May Concern: This is it. This is the recipe for my famous Walters Brew. Since'"—she paused to make out the next word—"'Emma'? Wait, no! *Edna*. 'Since Edna and I have no children, I don't know who to leave the recipe to. We talked it over and decided to hide it away in this closet and board the closet up. We thought it would be fun to let a future generation discover it.'"

"The secret room was just a closet?" Kaz said. He'd expected something more interesting.

"Sure is a BIG closet," Beckett said.

"So, what's in the recipe?" Claire's mom asked.

Claire turned to the second paper. "Allspice, birch bark, coriander, juniper, ginger, wintergreen, hops, sassafras root." She wrinkled her nose. "It's all weird stuff."

"Like any other soda-pop recipe," Grandma Karen said.

\* \* \* \* \* \* \* \* \* \* \* \* \* \* \*

The next day, Claire and her mom took the recipe to the historical society. Kaz and Little John traveled inside Claire's water bottle.

"This is it?" Mrs. Roman said eagerly when Claire pulled the papers out of the envelope. "This is the long-lost recipe?" She seemed afraid to even touch the paper.

"We think so. What do you think?" Claire's mom asked.

"We'll have our experts look it over, but it looks real to me," Mrs. Roman said. "Wherever did you find it after all these years?"

Claire bit her lip.

"We found it hidden behind a wall," Claire's mother said. Which was the truth, but not the whole truth.

"Oh, you must be doing some work in the library," Mrs. Roman said with a smile.

"A little," Claire's mom said.

"I still don't get why Claire and her mom don't want to tell that lady about us," Little John grumbled. "They never would've found that recipe if not for us."

"I already explained this to you," Kaz said. "A lot of solids don't believe in ghosts."

"That doesn't mean we don't exist," Little John said. "I could glow right now and show her we exist—"

"NO!" Kaz and Claire said at the same time.

"No what, dear?" Mrs. Roman asked Claire.

"Uh . . . ," Claire said. "No, we're not doing 'a little work' at the library. We're actually doing a lot of work. We're just doing it where people can't see."

Her mom nodded in agreement.

"Nice save," Kaz told Claire. He turned to his brother. "It's better if the solids don't know too much about us."

"Okay," Little John said with disappointment.

On the way back to the library, Claire asked her mom, "Can I help you and Dad with ghost cases from now on? Kaz still wants to find the rest of his family. Who knows? If someone has a ghost in their house, it could be Kaz's mom or dad or his big brother, Finn."

"Yes, we'll tell you about any ghost calls we get from now on," Claire's mom promised. "It's the least I can do to thank

your ghost friends for returning my doll. That doll was very special because my grandma made it. It's the only thing I have that she made."

"Speaking of grandparents," Kaz said. "When can you take us to visit *our* grandparents, Claire? I want to show them my transformation skills."

"We can do that right now," Claire said.

"Do what right now?" Claire's mom asked.

"Take Kaz and Little John to visit their grandparents," Claire said. "They live at the nursing home with a bunch of other ghosts. Can you drop us off?"

"A *bunch* of other ghosts?" Claire's mom's eyebrows shot up. "Just how many ghosts do you know, Claire?"

Claire laughed. "Oh, Mom. You have no idea!"